To: Scarlett
From: Grandma D.A.

Christmas 2021

WANTED
★ ★ ★
"FEARLESS"
oo READERS oo
and
WRITERS

Casey Rislov

**CASEY RISLOV BOOKS**
**WYOMING • USA**

To my mother Randy and my father Ronnie
for creating a life in the West that I will always call home
—C.D.R.

For all the cowboys and cowgirls who
tolerate the occasional horsefly
—Z.P.

Casey Rislov Books
2405 CY Avenue
Casper, WY 82604

www.caseyrislovbooks.com
caseyrislovbooks@gmail.com

Printed and bound in the United States of America
First Edition
10 9 8 7 6 5 4 3 2
LCCN 2018914347
ISBN 978-0-578-42945-8

This book was proudly produced by Book Bridge Press.
www.bookbridgepress.com

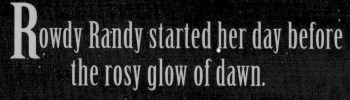

# Rowdy Randy started her day before the rosy glow of dawn.

She buzzed and buzzed from dawn till dusk.

Annoyance was her game, and she played it nonstop.

"I am the toughest cowgirl around," Randy boasted.

She was a sly lone ranger and preferred to work alone.

"Target straight ahead!"

Rowdy Randy swooped down and dove toward her first target.

An unsuspecting furry bandit! Randy couldn't resist.

The rascal's ears perked up. When it tried to nip her, Randy had to think again. "Maybe it's time to rethink my sneakin' ways."

Then she laughed and boasted,
"No one can match my stealthy moves."

"I am the greatest outlaw," Randy said.

Randy felt brazen from her first close call of the day.
She zipped away to look for another target.

She soon landed on a hilltop between two trees.
But Randy didn't settle for long.

As the sun's first peek of light started to show,
her restless eyes saw everywhere.

"Buzz!" and off she flew toward the shimmering shallows.

Randy flew low and eyed a slippery scoundrel.
The lively leaper launched right at her!

Randy bucked left, then she bucked right, like a rodeo daredevil,
narrowly escaping the cunning critter.

"Ha!" she laughed. "Thank you for the shower."
Rowdy Randy was too tough for any tough day to get under her skin.

Randy sat for a spell and dried her wings in the bright morning sun.
Pondering her predicament she said, "A group of me is just what I need!"
and she buzzed off to find tenderfoots she could train.

She spied a wild-looking bunch of bandits feasting by the roadside.
"Is this the team of outlaws I've been lookin' for?"

She zipped up to them and stated haughtily, "I am the Duchess.
I am the toughest broncobuster 'round these parts."

But the bald creatures ignored her and went back to their roadside chow.

"So much for camaraderie," Randy said, undeterred.
"Out West a cowgirl settles her own problems."

Rowdy Randy hitched a ride on a tumbleweed and traveled on.

"What's this?" she said, spotting a spunky
horned creature through a cloud of dust.
"Ah! Here's my chance to prove
I'm the best buckaroo this side of Cheyenne."

Randy swooped down and held tight for an eight-second ride.

"Yeehaw!" she shouted to the wind.

## "I was born to buck!"

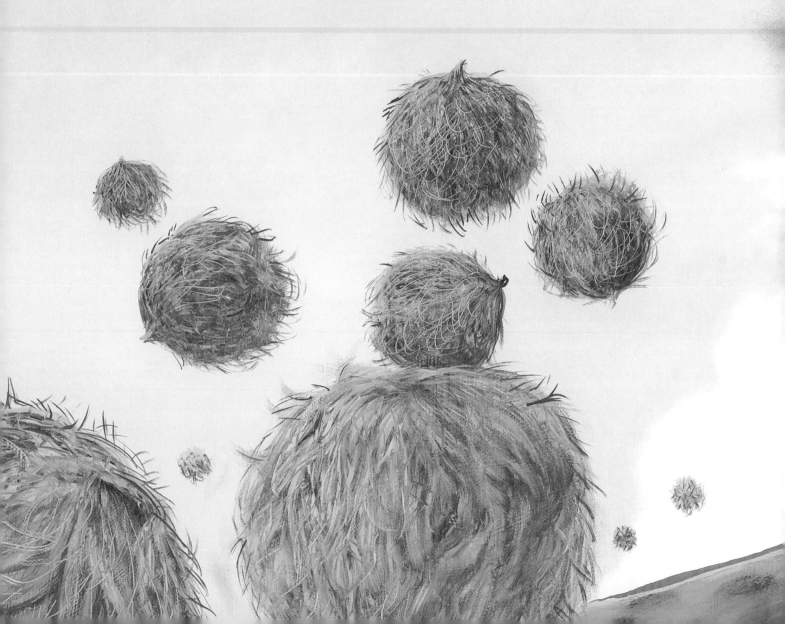

Rowdy Randy was feeling fine.
"Well, I think I've right proved my rumbling rodeo ways!"

But had Randy finally met her match?
Up ahead a herd of shaggy beasts grazed.

She darted toward the head of the herd. It didn't even flinch.

She boldly looked the dangerous desperado in the eyes and said,
"You gonna do somethin' about it?"

The brute answered with a stare-down.

Randy was unshaken, but zipped away,
figuring she best not press her luck.

"There's aplenty more Wild West to explore,"
Randy buzzed, weaving her way through the prairie grasses.

She zipped to a quick stop when she heard a rattling sound
that seemed to say "stay far away."

Randy had heard many a tale of this deadly creature.
"This will be my greatest challenge yet!"

But all her whooshing and buzzing only rustled up
more of the creature's slithery friends.

"The stakes are high," Randy said.
"I'll rope 'em next time." And off she zipped.

Driven by a fierce hunger and foolhardy pride,
Rowdy Randy grew more adventurous (some say dangerous)
with each encounter.

This diminutive desperado
had stirred up a heap of troubles along the way.

Randy had riled up a whole herd of wild-eyed rascals.

Legs and tails were everywhere.

Randy hollered at the rising dust bowl.

## "It's a full-blown stampede!"

Randy heard a "Whoa! Whoa!" behind her.

"Fellow broncobusters!" Randy said approvingly.
"They've got grit and speed just like me."

The wranglers rode hard,
commanding the whole stampede to a still.

Rowdy Randy wiped her brow
and declared her hard day's work done.

"I do believe I'll sit for a spot and cool my saddle," Randy said.

She strummed a ballad and gazed above at the shining stars.

*She was just a lonely cowgirl*

*with a heart so brave and true...*

She sang to her restless,
roaming spirit if to nobody else.

The cow camp seemed right peaceful
now as Randy crooned.

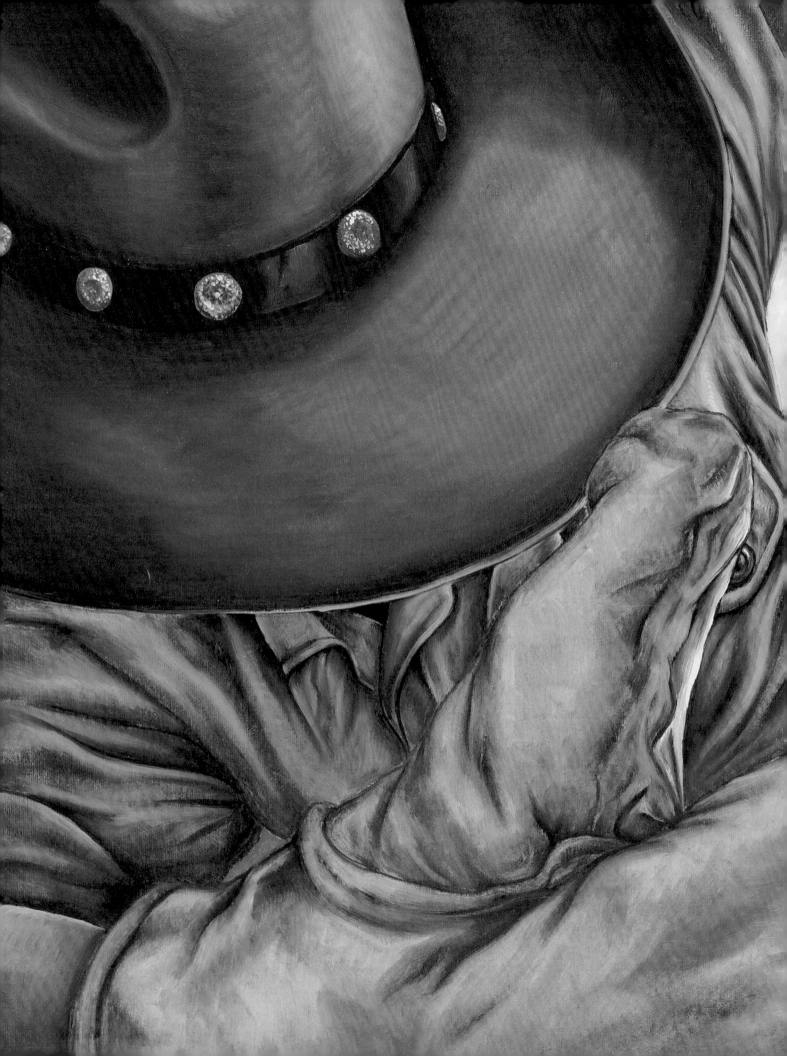

She had nearly lulled herself to sleep
when a large leather glove came out of nowhere.

It was headed her way!

## "Is this how it ends?"

CASEY DAY RISLOV has been sharing her love of reading and writing with young buckaroos since publishing her first children's book in 2011. She was bitten by the writing bug (much better than that time she was bitten by a horsefly!) and has published four more books since then. She loves her cowgirl life in Wyoming, where she lives with her three favorite cowboys. Learn more about Casey and her other books at caseyrislovbooks.com.

ZACHARY PULLEN'S picture-book illustrations have won awards and garnered starred reviews. He has been honored several times with acceptance into the prestigious Society of Illustrators juried shows and the Communication Arts: Illustration Annual, best in current illustration. Zak lives under the big blue skies of Wyoming with his wife Renate and son Hudson. See more of his work at zacharypullen.com.

If you have enjoyed this book...

We'd LOVE to hear from you
on Amazon or Goodreads